## Dear Parent:
## Your child's love of reading starts here!

Every child learns to read in a different way and at his or her own speed. Some go back and forth between reading levels and read favorite books again and again. Others read through each level in order. You can help your young reader improve and become more confident by encouraging his or her own interests and abilities. From books your child reads with you to the first books he or she reads alone, there are I Can Read Books for every stage of reading:

### SHARED READING
Basic language, word repetition, and whimsical illustrations, ideal for sharing with your emergent reader

### BEGINNING READING
Short sentences, familiar words, and simple concepts for children eager to read on their own

### READING WITH HELP
Engaging stories, longer sentences, and language play for developing readers

### READING ALONE
Complex plots, challenging vocabulary, and high-interest topics for the independent reader

### ADVANCED READING
Short paragraphs, chapters, and exciting themes for the perfect bridge to chapter books

I Can Read Books have introd                    :ading
since 1957. Featuring award-winn                 id a
fabulous cast of beloved characte
standard for beginning readers.

D0956643

A lifetime of discovery begins with the magical words **"I Can Read!"**

*Visit www.icanread.com for information*
*on enriching your child's reading experience.*

Fancy Nancy: The Case of the Disappearing Doll
Copyright © 2019 by Disney Enterprises, Inc.
All rights reserved. Printed in the United States of America.

ISBN 978-0-06-288868-6 (trade bdg.) —ISBN 978-0-06-284385-2 (pbk.)

Book design by Brenda E. Angelilli and Scott Petrower

19  20  21  22  23   LSCC   10  9  8  7  6  5

❖
First Edition

I Can Read!™ BEGINNING READING 1

Disney
Fancy NANCY

# The Case of the Disappearing Doll

Adapted by Nancy Parent
Based on the episode
by Laurie Israel

Illustrations by the
Disney Storybook
Art Team

**HARPER**
*An Imprint of HarperCollinsPublishers*

*Ooh la la!*

I am having a fancy tea party.

I set the table for my guests.

Mom is changing my bed.

"I have no idea how you find

anything in here," she says.

Bree and her doll Chiffon arrive.

I go to get my doll Marabelle.

Her doll bed is empty!

"Marabelle must be in her
dressing room," I say,
"or in her vacation *chateau*."
That's French for house.

I can't find Marabelle anywhere!

"She couldn't have disappeared
into thin air!" says Bree.

"If Marabelle is missing," I say,
"it can only mean one thing.
Someone took her!"

"Why would someone take Marabelle?" asks Bree. "Why? And who?" I say. "It's a mystery!"

We've got to solve

the Case of the Disappearing Doll.

"What do we do first?" asks Bree.

"Look for clues?"

"First we look like sleuths," I say.

That's fancy for people

who solve mysteries.

Bree and I go to the playhouse.

I look out the window

and see JoJo and Freddy.

"Maybe JoJo took Marabelle," I say.

"She's always taking my things."

"Let's interview JoJo!" I say.

That's fancy for asking

lots and lots of questions.

15

"Spill it," I tell JoJo.

"Did you take something
that wasn't yours?"

"How did you know?" asks JoJo.

"I ate your popcorn!" admits JoJo.

"I'm sorry!"

"I meant Marabelle," I say.

"Oh, I didn't take her," JoJo says.

We see Grace ride by on her bike.

"Is that a doll in Grace's basket?"

asks Bree.

Grace parks her bike.

I reach into Grace's bicycle basket.

"The jig is up!" I say.

That's fancy for gotcha!

"I know you took Marabelle!"

"Why would I take your doll?"
asks Grace.

"My doll was made to look like me."

"Of course," I say.

"I was just making sure."

Bree and I go back to my room.

I see a new clue on the floor.

"It's just a hair tie," says Bree.

"A tan, plain hair tie!" I say.

"Are you thinking . . ." asks Bree.

"Mom took Marabelle!" I say.

Bree and I hear noises

in the basement.

We go downstairs.

"I spend a lot of time
with Marabelle," I say.
"Maybe Mom is jealous!"
Mom's shadow is behind
a big bed sheet.

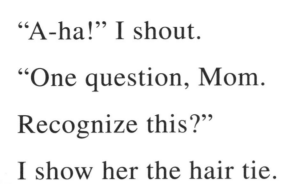

"A-ha!" I shout.

"One question, Mom.

Recognize this?"

I show her the hair tie.

"Oh thanks. It must have fallen out
when I was in your room," says Mom.
"When you were in there
taking Marabelle?" I ask.

"Sweetie, do you really think
I'd take your doll?" Mom asks.
"If you didn't take Marabelle,
then where is she?" I ask.
"We can't find her anywhere!"

"Where did you last see her?"

asks Mom.

"I got Marabelle out of bed,

changed for the tea party,

and put her on my bed . . ." I say.

27

"You took my bed sheets," I say.

"Maybe Marabelle is in the sheets!"

Bree and I look through

the laundry basket.

"She's not here!" I say.

"*Sacrebleu!* Oh no!" I say.

I see Marabelle in the washer.

Mom stops the washer

and opens the door.

I am so happy to see my doll!

"I'm sorry I blamed you," I say.

Mom gives me a hug.

She accepts my apology.

"Can we have our tea party now?"
asks Bree.

"*Oui*, yes!" I say.

"The Case of the Disappearing Doll
is closed!"

## Fancy Nancy's Fancy Words

These are the fancy words in this book:

*Chateau*—French for house

*Sleuths*—people who solve mysteries

*Interview*—to ask a lot of questions

*The jig is up*—gotcha

*Sacrebleu*—French for oh no

*Oui*—French for yes